Lucy the Diamond Fairy

by Daisy Meadows

illustrated by Georgie Ripper

Join the Rainbow Magic Reading Challenge!

Read the story and collect your fairy points to climb the Reading Rainbow online. Turn to the back of the book for details!

This book is worth 5 points.

The Jewel Fairies

To Holly Caitlin Powell, with lots of love

Special thanks to
Sue Mongredien

ORCHARD BOOKS

First published in Great Britain in 2005 by Orchard Books
This edition published in 2016 by The Watts Publishing Group

3 5 7 9 10 8 6 4

© 2016 Rainbow Magic Limited.
© 2016 HIT Entertainment Limited.
Illustrations © Georgie Ripper 2005

HiT entertainment

The moral rights of the author and illustrator have been asserted.
All characters and events in this publication, other than those clearly in the public domain,
are fictitious and any resemblance to real persons, living or dead, is purely coincidental.

A CIP catalogue record for this book is available from the British Library.

ISBN 978 1 40834 878 9

Printed and bound by CPI Group (UK) Ltd, Croydon, CR0 4YY

MIX
Paper from
responsible sources
FSC® C104740

FSC
www.fsc.org

The paper and board used in this book are made from wood from responsible sources

Orchard Books
An imprint of Hachette Children's Group
Part of The Watts Publishing Group Limited
Carmelite House, 50 Victoria Embankment, London EC4Y 0DZ

An Hachette UK Company
www.hachette.co.uk
www.hachettechildrens.co.uk

By Frosty magic I cast away
These seven jewels with their fiery rays,
So their magic powers will not be felt
And my icy castle shall not melt.

The fairies may search high and low
To find the gems and take them home.
But I will send my goblin guards
To make the fairies' mission hard.

Contents

A Musical Message

Kirsty Tate folded her jumper and put it into her bag. "There," she said to her best friend Rachel Walker. "I'm all packed." She looked at the clock on Rachel's bedroom wall. "Six o'clock already!" Kirsty groaned. "Mum and Dad will be here to pick me up soon. I can't believe this week is nearly over, can you?"

9

Rachel shook her head. "No," she replied. "It's gone so quickly. But it's been great fun."

The girls grinned at one another. Whenever they were together, the two of them always had the most wonderful adventures: fairy adventures! This week, while Kirsty had been staying with Rachel's family for half-term, the girls had been helping the Jewel Fairies find the seven missing magic jewels from Fairy Queen Titania's tiara!

Mean Jack Frost had stolen the gems, and, without them, some very important kinds of fairy magic were running low. So far, Kirsty and Rachel had found six of the stolen jewels – but the Diamond was still to be found.

Kirsty frowned. "I can't help feeling that something's wrong, today," she said. "I was sure we'd find the magic Diamond before I had to go home."

"Me, too," Rachel agreed. "And we haven't even seen a fairy yet. I wonder if they're all trapped in Fairyland."

The girls exchanged worried glances. They both knew that the Diamond controlled flying magic, and while it was missing, the fairies were starting to lose their ability to fly. The last fairy they'd seen, Sophie the Sapphire Fairy, had actually found her wings fading by the end of the day.

"We'll just have to find the Diamond and send it safely back to Fairyland by ourselves," Kirsty said in a determined voice. "Do you think we should start looking?"

Before Rachel could reply, both girls heard a delicate tinkling sound.

"It's your jewellery box," Kirsty said in surprise. "It's playing a tune all by itself!"

The girls rushed over to the jewellery

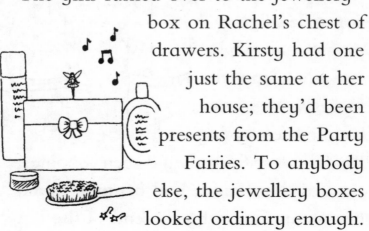

box on Rachel's chest of drawers. Kirsty had one just the same at her house; they'd been presents from the Party Fairies. To anybody else, the jewellery boxes looked ordinary enough.

Only Kirsty and Rachel knew that they had been made with a sprinkling of magical fairy dust.

"Listen," Rachel hissed. "I can hear singing!"

Both girls strained their ears to hear the faint sweet voices floating out of the jewellery box.

"Kirsty and Rachel, please come here. We need your help, that much is clear. Out of reach, though close at hand, The Diamond's here in Fairyland!"

Just as abruptly as it had started, the music stopped with a click.

Rachel's eyes were wide. "If the Diamond's in Fairyland, we need to be there too," she said.

Kirsty nodded and quickly opened the locket that she always wore around her neck. Queen Titania had given the girls matching lockets full of fairy dust which would take them straight to Fairyland if ever they needed help. "Let's use our last pinches of fairy dust to get there," she suggested.

"Good idea," Rachel agreed. "Let's go!"

Both girls sprinkled the glittering golden dust over themselves. Whoosh! There was a fizzing sound, then everything blurred into a whirlwind of sparkling rainbow colours. The girls felt as if they were tumbling through the air, shrinking smaller and smaller as they spun.

Moments later, they found themselves landing gently at the foot of a tall, twisting tree that stretched high above their heads.

There in front of them, stood King Oberon and Queen Titania, with all the Jewel Fairies.

"We're back in Fairyland," Kirsty cheered, "and we're fairies!" She flapped her shimmering wings happily. Being a fairy was such fun!

"Welcome back, girls," King Oberon said warmly.

"Hello," Rachel replied, smiling and feeling a thrill as she saw that almost all of the magical jewels were back in the Queen's tiara, and glittering brightly in the sun. But Rachel's smile faded as she suddenly realized that something was terribly wrong. "Your Majesties!" she gasped, looking around. "Where are all the fairies' wings?"

Starlight, Starbright

The Queen smiled sadly. "Thank you for coming, Kirsty and Rachel," she said. "As you can see, the Diamond's magic power has completely run out. Our wings grew fainter and fainter, and now they have vanished. None of us can fly!"

Kirsty's own wings trembled as she took in this shocking news. "But... but...we have wings," she said, feeling puzzled.

The King nodded. "That's because you've only just used your fairy dust. Its magic is still strong, but it won't last long."

A fairy with short, golden hair stepped forwards. She was wearing 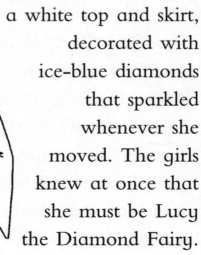 a white top and skirt, decorated with ice-blue diamonds that sparkled whenever she moved. The girls knew at once that she must be Lucy the Diamond Fairy.

"We think the Diamond is in the
Twisty Tree," she told the girls,
pointing to the towering tree beside
them. "Four goblins were spotted here
earlier today — and goblins never come
into Fairyland unless they're plotting
mischief."

"Do you think they were looking for
the Diamond?" Rachel asked.

Lucy nodded. "They spent ages bickering over who should climb the Twisty Tree to guard the Diamond," she went on. A twinkle came into her eye. "But this is the tallest tree in Fairyland and goblins don't like heights. After hours of arguing, they all decided to come back for guard duty tomorrow instead."

"So what's the plan?" Kirsty asked, gazing up at the tree. It really was tall, she marvelled, realising that its knotty trunk stretched up beyond the clouds and out of sight.

Lucy hesitated. "Well, I'd fly up and look for the Diamond myself, only…"

she looked over her shoulder at the spot where her wings used to be, "I can't," she finished sadly.

"Well, then, Rachel and I will fly up there and find the Diamond for you!" Kirsty declared firmly.

Lucy clapped her hands. "Oh, I was hoping you'd say that," she cried.

"Thank you, girls," the Queen added. "But please be very careful."

"We will," Rachel promised. "Come on, Kirsty. Let's get started."

The girls flapped their wings and set
off up the Twisty Tree as the Fairy
King and Queen headed back
to their palace. The tree
trunk was thick and
gnarled, and a tangle
of branches sprawled
out in all directions.
Kirsty and Rachel
searched along
every leafy branch,
carefully peeping
under all the leaves
and into all the scented
white blossoms. They
knew that Jack Frost had
wanted to keep the seven
magic jewels for himself, but he
had hurled them out of his castle in a

temper when he'd realized they were
too hot to keep in his ice palace.
It seemed that the
Diamond had hidden
itself in Fairyland.
Up and up the girls
went. Soon they had
flown right through
the fluffy, white
Fairyland clouds.
"I've seen lots of
bluebirds and
hundreds of silver
butterflies," Rachel
said after a while. "But
absolutely no diamonds!"
"Me too," Kirsty called
from higher up. "But Lucy
seemed sure it was here somewhere."

The girls continued their search, hoping to see a tell-tale sparkle, but eventually they found themselves at the very top of the tree, without having spotted any sign of the Diamond.

"Did we miss it, do you think?" Kirsty asked.

"I don't think so," Rachel replied, feeling disappointed. "We were looking so carefully." She shrugged. "We'd better fly down and tell Lucy we haven't found it, before our wings disappear too."

"I guess so," Kirsty sighed.

The sun was setting and the sky above Fairyland was turning from a beautiful pinky-orange to a deep red. Before Kirsty and Rachel had gone very far down the tree, the sky had darkened further to a purpley-blue.

"Look," Rachel said, hovering in mid-air as she gazed around her. "Fairyland stars. Aren't they pretty?"

Kirsty watched as the twinkling lights appeared in the warm evening darkness. "They're gorgeous," she breathed.

"Look at that one," Rachel said, pointing into the distance. "It's really bright."

Kirsty turned to see. The star was bigger and brighter than anything else in the sky. "It's different from the others," she remarked. "It looks almost as if it's shining with magic..."

Both girls gasped as the same thought hit them.

"The magic Diamond!" Kirsty cried.

"It's hidden in the sky with the stars!" Rachel finished.

A Frosty Encounter

Both girls zoomed towards the glittering
Diamond, which shone a brilliant white
in the velvety blue darkness. Kirsty
noticed that this jewel was smaller than
the others she and Rachel had found.
In the human world, the gems had been
as big as eggs. But here in Fairyland,
the Diamond was a fairy-sized jewel,

no bigger than an apple pip – though
of course it seemed bigger now that
Rachel and Kirsty were fairy-sized, too.

Kirsty stretched out her hand to grab
the shining gem as she drew closer. But
just before her fingers touched it, an icy
wind sprang up out of nowhere,
blowing her and Rachel away from
the Diamond.

"Help!" Kirsty cried, as the wind sent both girls tumbling through the sky, unable to fly at all. Luckily, they were swept into the boughs of the Twisty Tree, where they clung gratefully to the branches as the wind howled around them.

"Where did this storm come from?" Kirsty shivered, huddling closer to Rachel.

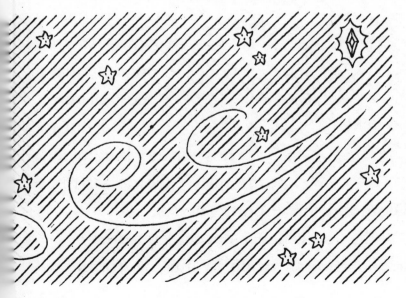

Rachel frowned as the wind moaned through the branches. "It feels like a magic storm," she said. "I wonder—" But before Rachel could finish her sentence, both girls heard a nasty laugh. "Jack Frost!" gasped Kirsty, as a dark, spiky figure zoomed towards them on a wintry blast of air. The bad fairy bowed mockingly to the girls. "Come for the Diamond, have you?" he sneered. "Well, you'll never get it. You aren't strong enough to fly in my ice storm!"

And, with that, Jack Frost pointed his glittering wand at the girls and sent an icy lightning bolt hurtling towards them.

The lightning crackled as it shot through the air and Rachel and Kirsty only just managed to throw themselves out of the way in time. The ice bolt struck the tree trunk nearby, and frost crystals glittered in its wake.

"Hurry!" Kirsty hissed. "We can't fly, but we can climb back down the tree. Come on!"

Rachel followed her friend. "We'll have to tell Lucy what's happened," she said, clambering down the trunk as quickly as she could.

"And think of a way to get the Diamond away from horrible Jack Frost," Kirsty added in a low voice, climbing down through the clouds.

The thick, fluffy cloud layer seemed to be shielding the air below from Jack Frost's storm. As Kirsty and Rachel emerged underneath, they were relieved to find that the air was calmer and they were able to fly the rest of the way to the ground.

Lucy was waiting for them. "Are you all right?" she asked at once.

Kirsty quickly told her what had happened. Lucy cheered at the news that they'd found the Diamond, but when Kirsty told her that Jack Frost was guarding the jewel, Lucy groaned.

"Jack Frost is far harder to outwit than his stupid goblins," she sighed, frowning thoughtfully.

"So, what can we do?" Rachel asked.

"Maybe if Rachel and I distract Jack Frost," Kirsty said slowly, "somebody else could sneak up and grab the Diamond while he isn't looking. What a shame we haven't got any fairy dust left. Lucy, is there any fairy at all who is still strong enough to fly?"

Lucy shook her head sadly and the three friends fell silent, trying to think of a plan to outwit Jack Frost.

Then, suddenly, a smile appeared on Lucy's face and she started dancing up and down. "That's it! Of course!" she laughed. "Kirsty – you're a genius!"

Fairy Friends to the Rescue

"I am?" Kirsty replied, looking baffled.

"Yes – because Pegasus will help us!" Lucy cried. She grinned at the girls' blank expressions. "He's a winged horse who lives right here in Fairyland, and he's lovely. I'll see if I can call him with a spell."

Kirsty and Rachel waited excitedly as Lucy waved her wand with a flourish, sending ice-white sparkles spiralling up into the air. After just a moment, the girls felt a great wind whip up around them and they looked nervously up at the sky, fearing that Jack Frost was on his way. But both girls gasped in delight, because there, beating his great, white feathered wings, was a silvery-white flying horse!

Pegasus whinnied softly as he landed beside Lucy and nuzzled her shoulder.

The little fairy stroked his silky white mane. "Oh, Pegasus, thank you for coming," she said. "We need your help!"

As Lucy told Pegasus what was happening, neither Kirsty nor Rachel could take their eyes off the graceful winged horse. His mane and tail gleamed silver in the starlight, and his body seemed to glow with a magical white light.

Then Pegasus nodded his great head
and stamped a foot.
"He'll do it!" Lucy
cried, and threw her
arms around his neck.
"I knew he'd help."
She beamed at the
girls as she climbed
onto Pegasus's back.

"Now, while you two distract Jack
Frost, Pegasus and I will fly up behind
him and get the Diamond," Lucy
declared.

"Hooray!" cried Kirsty. "Let's go!"

Kirsty, Rachel and Pegasus all flapped
their wings and flew up into the dark
night sky through the clouds. Lucy
waved her wand, sending a stream of
sparkling white stars ahead to light

their way.

Kirsty and Rachel looked nervously
at one another as they approached
the Diamond. "Come on," Kirsty said,
grabbing Rachel's hand. "We can do
this. We've got to — for the sake of
the fairies!"

The two friends flew on. Here above
the clouds, the air was cold but calm
again now.

"There's Jack Frost," Rachel hissed, seeing him whizzing around between the stars. "Are you ready?"

Kirsty nodded. "Ready," she said.

The girls flew towards Jack Frost.

"Having another go, are we?" he taunted, when he spotted them. "Well, you'll never get past me."

"We're not scared of you!" Rachel called out loudly. "You're nothing but hot air, Mr Jack Frost!"

Jack Frost gave a gleeful cackle. "Hot air, did you say?" he asked. "Well, this should cool you down!" He stretched out a bony finger and several bolts of magic ice lightning shot from his hand, and flew straight towards Kirsty and Rachel!

Danger in the Stars

Kirsty and Rachel swerved aside in alarm, and the lightning bolts thudded into the Twisty Tree behind them with a deafening crash.

Rachel's heart pounded in fear, but she was determined not to give up. "We've got to keep him distracted," she muttered. "Come on, Kirsty."

The girls bravely flew on towards Jack Frost.

"Haven't you learned your lesson yet?" he cried.

Another lightning bolt zigzagged towards the girls. They both veered away and it, too, whacked into the tree, knocking a branch clean off the trunk. Kirsty gulped. The ice lightning had come so close to her, she had felt its freezing fire whistle past her wings.

Once again, though, she and Rachel turned back to face their enemy. And then, to her great delight, Kirsty saw Pegasus galloping through the night sky behind Jack Frost, with Lucy clinging to his silvery mane. Kirsty heard Rachel gasp with excitement and realized that she, too, had seen the Diamond Fairy. Now Kirsty knew she had to make sure Jack Frost didn't take his eyes off herself and Rachel for a second!

"Missed us," Kirsty sang out as defiantly as she could. "You need to get your eyes tested, Jack Frost; you're not throwing straight."

Jack Frost let out a thunderous roar of rage. "That does it!" he bellowed. "This time, I'll knock you pesky girls out of the sky!"

But as he started muttering a spell, Kirsty saw that behind him Pegasus and Lucy had reached the Diamond. Lucy plucked it out of the night sky and gave the girls a thumbs-up sign. Then Pegasus galloped away, his powerful wings beating strongly.

But Jack Frost heard the sound of
Pegasus's wing beats and
he broke off from his
spell. "What's that?"
he cried
suspiciously.
He turned and
let out a yell
of fury as he
spotted Lucy on
the winged horse,
and realized that
he'd been tricked.
"Come back!" he
roared, pointing his
wand at Pegasus.

The magical horse neighed and
tossed his head defiantly as a freezing
bolt of lightning hurtled towards him.

Pegasus dodged the bolt neatly, but had to swerve so sharply that Lucy almost lost her balance. She clutched at his mane to keep herself from falling, but in doing so, lost her grip on the Diamond. Rachel and Kirsty watched in horror as the precious jewel tumbled through the air.

"I'll get it!" Kirsty yelled, diving towards the Diamond as it fell. She flung out a hand, stretching to reach the jewel. "Yes!" she cried triumphantly, as her fingers closed around the gem. "Got it!"

Jack Frost snarled. "Oh, no, you don't!" he shouted, calling out a spell.

Kirsty gasped as she suddenly felt her wings freeze and go numb. Jack Frost's spell had turned them to ice; she could no longer fly.

"Help!" screamed Kirsty, trying desperately to flap her icy wings. But it was no good, they were frozen solid. And now she was falling, with the Diamond still clutched in her hand.

"Hold on, I'm coming," Rachel cried, swooping towards her friend as fast as she could fly.

Jack Frost pointed his wand at her, too, and a flood of icy sparkles chased after Rachel. But Rachel managed to dodge his magic, and zoomed after Kirsty at top speed. She grabbed Kirsty's hand, flapping her wings as hard as she could to try and drag her friend upwards with her, but it was hopeless. Rachel's wings just weren't strong enough to carry two fairies. Try as she might, Rachel soon found herself and Kirsty sinking faster and faster towards the ground.

Jack Frost laughed nastily, and Rachel thought that she and Kirsty were doomed to crash, but suddenly, Lucy and Pegasus were there, swooping beneath the girls.

Rachel and Kirsty landed with a jolt on the horse's back.

"Oh, well done, Pegasus!" Kirsty gasped in relief. "And I've still got the Diamond!" she added.

"Take us to the royal palace,
Pegasus." Lucy urged.

Rachel felt an icy blast behind her,
and turned to see Jack Frost
chasing after them.

"Quick, Pegasus!"
she squealed.
"Fly as fast
as you can!"

With Jack
Frost closing
in on them,
Pegasus
surged
through
the cloud
layer and into
the warmer skies
above Fairyland.

Kirsty peered downwards and saw the royal palace below, with King Oberon, Queen Titania and the other six Jewel Fairies waiting in the courtyard.

"Hold out the Diamond, Kirsty," Lucy called, and as Kirsty stretched out her hand, Lucy touched the end of her wand to the magic jewel.

In a fountain of sparks, the Diamond vanished. But as Pegasus landed and the three friends slid off his silvery back, it reappeared, shining like a star in Queen Titania's tiara.

At once, magic in every colour of the rainbow sparkled around the Fairy Queen, and she smiled at Kirsty and Rachel. "Well done, girls," she called in her soft, musical voice as she undid Jack Frost's spell on Kirsty's wings.

But at that moment, a terrible
howl of rage came from Jack Frost.
He had followed Pegasus through
the clouds and was now hovering
in the sky overhead. "You girls
have ruined everything!" he
thundered, and waved his wand in
a complicated pattern.

Instantly, the air turned bitterly
cold, an icy wind sprang up and
chased away the clouds, and,
above, the Fairyland stars seemed
to tremble.

Kirsty looked up and screamed in
fear, because showers of glittering,
razor-sharp icicles were raining down
on her and Rachel.

Fire and Ice

Swiftly, Queen Titania lifted her own wand. Magic crackled from the tip in golden sparks, which flew to meet the icicles. As the fiery sparks touched the ice, the icicles were transformed into rainbow-coloured sparkles which drifted down harmlessly around the girls.

"NOOO!" shouted Jack Frost angrily, and swung his wand in the direction of the Queen. At once a freezing ice-wind came rushing towards her.

Queen Titania's wand flashed in the sky as she cast another spell and sent a stream of rainbow-coloured magic shooting towards Jack Frost. As the girls watched, the Queen's magic collided with the ice-wind, and there was a huge explosion that lit up the night sky with vivid streaks of rainbow colours.

"It's like fireworks!"
Rachel gasped.

"And look,
Queen Titania's
spell is stronger!"
Kirsty cheered,
watching as the
rainbow colours
of the Queen's
spell forced Jack
Frost's ice-white
magic hurtling
back upon him.

Jack Frost shouted in shock and fury
as he was sent spinning and tumbling
through the night sky by his own icy
gale. The girls watched his figure
grow smaller and smaller as he spun
away into the distance.

"That should take him far enough away to keep him out of trouble for a while," the Queen said with satisfaction. Then she turned to Rachel and Kirsty. "My dear girls," she said, taking their hands. "You've saved Fairyland again — and with such a daring rescue! I can't tell you how good it is to have my tiara complete with all its jewels again."

"You were wonderful," Lucy added, hugging the girls. And the other six Jewel Fairies rushed over to thank Kirsty and Rachel, too.

"Now we must recharge everybody's magic supply!" the Queen announced. "And Kirsty and Rachel will be our very special guests for the ceremony," she added. "Take your places, fairies."

Kirsty and Rachel watched as the royal band, including their friend, Bertram the frog footman, emerged from the palace and struck up a ceremonial march. At once, fairies started coming from all directions, laughing and cheering as they lined up behind the King and Queen.

The Queen beckoned Rachel and Kirsty to join her, as she and the King led the procession into the palace.

"This is so exciting," Kirsty breathed as they marched through the Great Hall. "I hope it isn't just a lovely dream that India has sent me!"

The procession entered a small chamber, and the girls held their breath as the Queen took off her tiara and placed it on a red velvet cushion.

Instantly, a fountain of
sparkling light shot
up from each
jewel, and met in
mid-air above the
tiara to form a
twinkling rainbow
of fairy dust.

"Wow!" Rachel
exclaimed. "It's so beautiful!"

The King and Queen dipped their
wands into the rainbow, and the tips
glowed brightly. Then Lucy did the
same, and a faint outline of her wings
reappeared on her back, growing brighter
and stronger until her wings shimmered
and shone with pure, sparkly fairy magic.

One by one, every fairy in the
procession did the same, recharging their

wands with the power
of the jewels' magic.
And as their wings
reappeared, each
fairy's face lit
up in delight.
"Look!" Kirsty said,
nudging Rachel. The two
girls peeped out of the window to see the
courtyard outside the palace filling with
happy fairies, fluttering and flying
loop-the-loops just for fun.

When all the fairies had recharged
their wands, the King and Queen led
Rachel and Kirsty out into the
courtyard, too. There was so much
magic in the air, it was positively
fizzing with rainbow coloured sparks
from all the fairy wands.

"Thank you again for all your hard work, girls," the King said, smiling. "We would like you to have these as a token of our thanks." And he handed each girl a beautiful ring.

"Thank you," Rachel said, slipping it onto her finger where it fitted perfectly, of course. "Look, Kirsty, in the rings are all the gems of the Queen's tiara: moonstone, garnet, emerald, topaz, sapphire, amethyst and diamond!"

"Every time I wear this ring, I'll remember the adventures we've had with the Jewel Fairies," Kirsty said happily.

Then the Queen touched her wand to

each of the girls' golden lockets. "I've refilled your lockets with fairy dust," she said, "so that you can come and find us, if ever you need our help." She hugged both girls warmly. "And now, it's home time."

"Thank you for everything," Rachel and Kirsty chorused, as the King waved his wand in the air and a haze of rainbow sparkles swirled around them. At once, the fairies' laughter faded and Rachel and Kirsty found themselves back in Rachel's bedroom.

"Oh, Kirsty," Rachel cried, gazing at her fairy ring. "What an adventure!"

Kirsty nodded, but before she could speak, there was a knock at the front door.

"We're just in time! Mum and Dad must be here," Kirsty said, tucking her fairy ring safely into her bag.

"What a brilliant week," Rachel sighed. "I can't wait until the next time we're together."

Kirsty nodded happily. "Who knows what fairy adventures we'll have then!" she laughed.

The two friends grinned at each other and hurried downstairs to the front door.

Now it's time for Kirsty and Rachel to help...

Katie the Kitten Fairy

Read on for a sneak peek...

"Catch!"

Kirsty Tate hurled a tennis ball into the air and watched as her friend Rachel Walker ran across the grass to catch it. It was the first day of the Easter holidays and Rachel had come to stay with Kirsty's family for a whole week. The two girls were in the park while Kirsty's parents were at the supermarket. With the sun shining brightly and no trace of a cloud in the sky, it felt like perfect holiday weather.

Rachel held up the ball triumphantly.

"Your turn," she called. "Ready?"

Before Kirsty could reply, there was a loud sound of barking, and both girls spun around to see a large black dog thundering past them.

Rachel jumped back quickly as the dog raced by. "Is that a squirrel it's chasing?" she asked, staring after it.

Kirsty shielded her eyes from the sun for a better look. "No, it's a kitten!" she exclaimed...

Read Katie the Kitten Fairy to find out what adventures are in store for Kirsty and Rachel!

Calling all parents, carers and teachers!
The Rainbow Magic fairies are here to help
your child enter the magical world of reading.
Whatever reading stage they are at, there's
a Rainbow Magic book for everyone!
Here is Lydia the Reading Fairy's guide to
supporting your child's journey at all levels.

Starting Out

Our Rainbow Magic Beginner Readers are perfect for first-time readers who are just beginning to develop reading skills and confidence. Approved by teachers, they contain a full range of educational levelling, as well as lively full-colour illustrations.

1

Developing Readers

Rainbow Magic Early Readers contain longer stories and wider vocabulary for building stamina and growing confidence. These are adaptations of our most popular Rainbow Magic stories, specially developed for younger readers in conjunction with an Early Years reading consultant, with full-colour illustrations.

2

Going Solo

The Rainbow Magic chapter books – a mixture of series and one-off specials – contain accessible writing to encourage your child to venture into reading independently. These highly collectible and much-loved magical stories inspire a love of reading to last a lifetime.

3

www.rainbowmagicbooks.co.uk

"Rainbow Magic got my daughter reading chapter books. Great sparkly covers, cute fairies and traditional stories full of magic that she found impossible to put down" – Mother of Edie (6 years)

"Florence LOVES the Rainbow Magic books. She really enjoys reading now" – Mother of Florence (6 years)

Read along the Reading Rainbow!

Well done – you have completed the book!

This book was worth 1 star.

See how far you have climbed on the Reading Rainbow.
The more books you read, the more stars you can colour in
and the closer you will be to becoming a Royal Fairy!

Do you want to print your own Reading Rainbow?

1) Go to the Rainbow Magic website

2) Download and print out the poster

3) Colour in a star for every book you finish
and climb the Reading Rainbow

4) For every step up the rainbow,
you can download your very own certificate

There's all this and lots more at
rainbowmagicbooks.co.uk

You'll find activities, stories, a special newsletter
AND you can search for the fairy with your name!